Fairest Rose

Kenzie Skye

ONE

The clock's hands seem to be moving at a glacial pace as I lean against the counter, absently wiping down the already spotless surface. The Poisoned Apple Café is empty now, the last customer having left fifteen minutes ago in a jingle of bells above the door. I'm just waiting to close up while outside, the city streets are bathed in the warm glow of the setting sun, casting long shadows across the cobblestones. I can hear the distant laughter and chatter of people enjoying the start of their evening, and a pang of longing shoots through me.

What I wouldn't give to be out there among them, breathing in the crisp autumn air and letting the stress of the day melt away. Instead, I'm stuck here, trapped by the responsibilities of running my family's café. It's not that I don't love The Poisoned Apple—I do, with all my heart. But sometimes, the weight of my legacy feels like a heavy cloak draped across my shoulders, suffocating me with its expectations.

I sigh, my gaze drifting to the antique mirror hanging on the wall behind the counter. My reflection stares back at me, blue eyes tinged with weariness and a hint of something else—a restless yearning for more than this mundane existence. The discovery of the old diary in the attic has only intensified this feeling, awakening a part of me I never knew existed. The secrets it contains whisper to me in the stillness of the night, promising a world of magic and wonder beyond the confines of this café.

But that world seems so far away, a distant dream that I can barely grasp. The reality is this: the endless cycle of baking, serving, and cleaning, day after day.

The bell above the door jingles, drawing my attention from the heart I'm swirling into a latte. I glance up, expecting one of my regulars, but instead find myself captivated by striking green eyes I've never seen before. He walks toward the counter with an easy grace, like a panther stalking through shadows.

"Welcome to The Poisoned Apple," I say, my voice steadier than my suddenly racing heart. "What can I get for you?"

He stares at me for a long moment—so long that I start to fidget, wondering if I've got something on my face.

But then I stare back into his eyes...There's something about him that draws me in, a magnetic pull that I can't quite explain. It's as if he sees through the façade I present to the world, straight into the depths of my soul.

His lips quirk into a lopsided smile. "Surprise me."

I cock an eyebrow. "Feeling adventurous, are we?"

"Always." His gaze lingers on me, enigmatic yet alluring.

As I craft his drink, I feel the weight of his stare, sending tingles across my skin. Who is this mystery man? And why do I feel this inexplicable pull toward him, like gravity shiftingon its axis?

"Here you go." I slide the mug across to him, our fingers brushing. Electricity zings through me at the contact. "A blueberry lavender mocha with a twist. Careful, it's got a bite."

"I think I can handle it," he murmurs, holding my gaze as he takes a sip. "I'm Evan, by the way."

"Snow." I absently tuck a raven lock behind my ear, caught in his magnetic pull.

The air between us crackles with an undeniable tension, a sizzling current that sets my nerves alight. Evan leans in closer, his breath warm against my cheek as he murmurs, "Snow. A name as enchanting as the woman herself."

Heat flares across my skin at his proximity, desire coiling low in my belly. I swallow hard, trying to regain my composure, but it's a losing battle. "Quite the charmer, aren't you?" I manage, my voice husky.

"Only with those who captivate me." His fingertips graze along my jaw, leaving trails of fire in their wake. "And you, Snow, have utterly bewitched me."

I lick my suddenly dry lips, my gaze dropping to his mouth. The urge to taste him consumes me, to lose myself in his embrace and forget the weight of the world for a little while. "You don't even know me," I whisper, even as I sway toward him, drawn in by an irresistible force.

"But I want to." Evan's hand slides around to cup the back of my neck, his touch searing through me. "I want to unravel every delicious secret hidden beneath your beautiful surface."

A whimper escapes me as he closes the remaining distance, his lips claiming mine in a searing kiss. I melt into him, my fingers tangling in his silky hair as our mouths move together in a sensual dance. He tastes of blueberries and sin, intoxicating me with each sweep of his clever tongue.

Evan's hands roam my curves, igniting flames wherever they touch. He lifts me effortlessly onto the counter, settling between my thighs as he deepens the kiss. I wrap my legs around his waist, grinding against the thick ridge of his arousal. Wanton moans fill the air, the sounds of our passion echoing in the empty café.

"I need you," Evan growls against my throat, his teeth grazing my racing pulse. "Need to feel your tight little cunt wrapped around my cock."

His crude words only fan the flames higher, my core clenching with desperate need. "Then take me," I breathe, too far gone to care about propriety. "Fuck me, Evan. Make me forget everything but your name."

With a groan, he yanks my panties aside and sinks two fingers deep into my dripping heat. I cry out, my head falling back as he strokes me expertly, stoking the inferno raging inside me. "So fucking wet for me already," he rumbles, his thumb circling my clit. "Such a dirty girl, aren't you Snow? Gonna look so pretty split open on my dick."

I can only keen in response, my hips rocking shamelessly against his hand. Evan curses, withdrawing his fingers to fumble with his zipper. Then he's freeing his rigid length from its confines.

A strangled gasp escapes me as Evan's thick length springs free, long and hard and absolutely mouthwatering. He strokes himself slowly, emerald eyes burning into mine with raw hunger. "Like what you see, beautiful?"

I lick my lips, transfixed by the bead of moisture glistening at his tip. "God, yes. I want to taste you," I breathe, reaching for him.

Evan captures my wrist, pinning it above my head as he leans in to nip at my bottom lip. "Later. Right now, I'm going to bury myself so deep inside your sweet cunt you'll be feeling me for days."

His filthy promise sends a gush of arousal flooding my core. Evan notches himself at my entrance, the broad head of his cock nudging my slick folds. With one powerful thrust, he sheaths himself to the hilt, stretching me deliciously around his thick girth.

"Fuck!" I cry out, my back arching off the counter as he fills me completely.

"That's it, Snow. Take every fucking inch," Evan growls, his hips pistoning in a relentless rhythm. Each deep stroke hits that magic spot inside me, stars bursting behind my eyelids.

I cling to his broad shoulders, my nails digging into his skin as he pounds into me. The obscene slap of flesh against flesh mingles with our ragged moans, the scent of sex heavy in the air. Evan's hand snakes between our sweat-slicked bodies, his fingers finding my aching clit.

"Come for me," he commands roughly, rubbing the sensitive bundle of nerves. "Squeeze my cock like the greedy little thing you are."

His dirty talk catapults me to the edge. With a hoarse scream, I shatter, my pussy clamping down on him like a vice. Evan buries his face in my neck, muffling his shout as my rippling walls milk him of his own release.

We stay locked together, chests heaving, pulses gradually slowing. After a long moment, Evan carefully withdraws, leaving me feeling strangely bereft. He tucks a damp curl behind my ear, his touch infinitely tender compared to seconds before.

"That was..." I struggle to find words, my sex-clouded brain sluggish.

"Incredible," he finishes, his lips curling into a

satisfied smirk. "And only the beginning, Snow. I meant what I said—I fully intend to unravel your every secret. In more ways than one."

Despite the bone-deep satisfaction thrumming through me, a flicker of unease stirs at his cryptic words. Who exactly is this magnetic stranger? And what does he truly want from me, beyond the physical?

Before I can gather my thoughts enough to ask, the clock chimes the hour, breaking the spell. Reality crashes back down around me.

I blink, and he's gone. My mouth falls open.

What the—? *Was it all just my imagination?*

But, I mean, surely it had to be because what stranger just walks into a coffee shop and has sex with the worker right there where anyone could walk in? Maybe I dozed off. Maybe I'm so bored, my imagination is overactive.

I don't know, but surely that couldn't have *really* happened.

Could it?

I shake my head and move to close up. I need some rest. I'm obviously going insane from boredom.

As I'm closing up, a glint catches my eye—a brass key peeking out from behind a loose brick in the wall. Curious, I wiggle it free, the metal cool against my palm.

Twisting the key, a panel swings open to reveal a narrow staircase, leading up into shadowy heights. My heartbeat quickens. All these years and I never knew this was here!

Grabbing a flashlight, I ascend the creaking steps, dust motes swirling in the beam of light.

At the top, I find myself in a small attic room. Antique furniture huddles under sheets, and an ornate chest beckons from the corner.

Inside, nestled in crimson velvet, rests a weathered leather-bound book. Hands trembling, I lift it out and trace the gold-leafed words on the cover: "Secrets of the Sorceress."

I sink onto the floor and flip it open, yellowed pages releasing the scent of history. Elegant script dances across the paper, detailing a lineage descending from a coven of powerful witches. Story after story of rituals, spells, and a chauvinist blood feud with a sinister warlock who cursed our line.

As I turn the pages, a polaroid flutters out—and I gasp. The woman in the picture is a mirror image of me, down to the constellation of freckles on our noses. Hands shaking, I flip it over and read:

My darling Snow, if you're reading this, then the darkness I've feared has risen once more. Trust your power, trust your heart. The truth is in your blood. You are the last daughter of winter, and only you can break the curse. Find the emerald key. Believe, my dear girl. I am with you, always.

-Nanna

My grandmother? I turn back to the front of the book and see her name inscribed on the inside page.

Oh my god...

Tears blur the smiling face as realization crashes through me. Magic is *real*. Witches are *real*. And apparently, *I'm* one of them. Fear and exhilaration tangle in my chest. What does this mean? What curse? What darkness?

I'm so absorbed, I almost miss the soft creak of a footstep behind me. I whirl around, flashlight beam landing on a tall figure in the shadows. My heart leaps into my throat.

Then *he* steps into the light and I see those unforgettable green eyes—Evan.

He's real too. I blush.

Then, that means...we really did...

His gaze drops to the open book in my hands. When he looks back up at me, there's a glimmer of understanding...and something else. Something ancient and feral.

"So, you've finally awakened, little witch. The game begins."

Two

The air crackles with tension as Evan's words hang between us, heavy with unspoken secrets. I clutch the diary tighter, as if it could shield me from the intensity of his gaze.

"Game? What game? What do you know about all this?" The questions tumble out, my voice trembling slightly.

He takes a step closer, and I instinctively back up until I feel the rough brick wall behind me. Evan tilts his head, a slight smile playing at the corners of his mouth. "Oh, Snow. There's so much you don't know. So much power lurking beneath your skin, waiting to be unleashed."

His fingertips graze my cheek, sending a shiver

down my spine. Fear and something else, something dangerous and alluring, coil in my stomach.

I swallow hard. "Tell me. Please."

He leans in, his breath warm against my ear. "Your stepmother, Evelyn? She's not who you think she is. She's the one who cursed your family, who's been hiding the truth from you all these years."

I feel like I've been punched in the gut. Evelyn, the woman who raised me after Mom died, who's always been distant but never cruel...a witch? It can't be.

But even as denial rises in my throat, pieces start clicking into place. The way she always keeps her study locked, the strange herbs I've caught glimpses of, how her eyes sometimes seem to flash an unearthly green...

Evan must sense my racing thoughts because he cups my face, forcing me to meet his gaze. "She knows, Snow. She knows you're awakening, and she'll do anything to stop you from claiming your birthright."

Birthright. The word sears into my mind, igniting a spark of anger amid the fear and confusion. If magic is my legacy, my truth, I won't let anyone, not even Evelyn, take that from me.

I straighten my spine, my voice hardening with resolve. "What do I need to do?"

Evan's smile widens, sharp and full of dark promise. "Embrace your power. Find the emerald key. Break the curse."

He steps back, melting into the shadows as quickly as he appeared.

And I'm left alone in the attic, pulse pounding, the diary clutched to my chest like a lifeline.

Evelyn's heels click on the floorboards downstairs, a sound that once brought comfort, now laced with trepidation. I have to confront her.

But first, I need to learn exactly what I'm capable of. I glance down at my hands, wondering what magic might flow through these veins.

THREE

I step out of the café into the crisp evening air, lost in thought. A gust of wind catches me off guard, blowing stray locks of raven hair across my face. As I brush them away, I collide with a solid form. Strong hands grasp my arms to steady me.

"We have to stop meeting like this," a familiar voice teases. I look up into Evan's emerald eyes, sparkling with amusement. My breath catches.

"Maybe you should watch where you're going," I retort, trying to ignore the sparks shooting through me at his touch. Why does he unsettle me so?

He smiles enigmatically. "Maybe it's fate."

I scoff, pulling away. "I don't believe in fate. We make our own choices."

"Do we?" He studies me intently, as if trying to

unravel my secrets. "Sometimes I think there are forces at work beyond our control, Snow. Drawing certain people together..."

His words hang in the air between us, heavy with unspoken meaning. I shiver, wrapping my arms around myself. "That sounds like a fancy way of avoiding responsibility for your actions."

"Or maybe an acknowledgement that there are things in this world we can't explain." He takes a step closer, voice low. "Haven't you ever felt a connection with someone you can't quite understand? Like they're meant to be in your life?"

Yes. With you. The unbidden thought startles me. I shake my head, backing away. "I should go. Early day tomorrow and all that."

Evan nods, disappointment flickering across his chiseled features. "Of course. Sleep well, Snow White." He turns and strides off into the night, leaving me chilled and confused in ways that have nothing to do with the cool air.

I hurry home to my empty apartment above the café, mind churning. I can't deny the pull I feel toward Evan, but I also can't afford distractions. I've got to figure out this magic thing....

Evan is a mystery, but he's not one I'm not sure I should try to solve.

If only my traitorous heart would listen to reason. With a sigh, I climb into bed, willing sleep to quiet my racing thoughts. But even in dreams, I cannot escape those fathomless green eyes...

———

Miles away in a manor cloaked in darkness, Evelyn glides down an empty hall, hair shimmering like burnished copper in the flickering torchlight. She pushes open a heavy wooden door, revealing a chamber draped in shadow.

In the center, an ornate mirror gleams, its surface swirling with opalescent mist. Evelyn approaches, skirts whispering across the stone floor.

"Mirror, mirror, on the wall," she purrs. "Who threatens my power most of all?"

The mist parts like a curtain, revealing a young woman with skin white as snow, lips red as blood, hair black as ebony. Evelyn's hand clenches into a fist.

"The girl is the key," the mirror intones, its voice ancient and hollow. "The last of her bloodline, heir to the old magic you seek to claim. And the prince...he could be her awakening. Their bond grows, despite his curse. If he breaks free—"

"He will not," Evelyn hisses, emerald eyes flashing.

"Snow White will never come into her power. I'll make certain of that."

The surface ripples, and the image fades. Evelyn turns away, lips curled in a frigid smile. "Sleep while you can, little princess," she whispers to the empty room. "For I'm coming for you..."

I awaken with a gasp.

Evenlyn...

The mirror...

It was me she was talking about.

Princess...prince...

I'm so confused.

———

The next morning, I drag myself into the café, exhaustion weighing heavily on my shoulders. The strange dream lingers in my mind like a dense fog, Evelyn's ominous words echoing in my ears. Princess? Prince? The concepts feel foreign, yet somehow familiar, like a long-forgotten melody.

I'm tying my apron when the bell above the door jingles. I glance up and freeze. Evelyn glides in, her auburn hair cascading down the back of her designer coat. She radiates an aura of power and sophistication that makes me feel small in comparison.

"Snow, darling," she greets me, her voice like honey laced with arsenic. "You look absolutely dreadful. Rough night?"

I force a smile, trying to shake off the unease her presence evokes. "Just didn't sleep well. What can I get for you, Evelyn?"

She studies me, her emerald eyes piercing through my defenses. "Oh, the usual. But first, I wanted to chat with you about something." She leans against the counter, her perfectly manicured nails tapping an idle rhythm. "Have you come across a man named Evan?"

My heart skips a beat at the mention of his name. How could she know about him? "What about him?" I ask, trying to keep my voice steady.

Evelyn's lips curve into a smile that doesn't reach her eyes. "I've seen him around town, you know. Always with a different girl on his arm. Quite the charmer, that one." She laughs, a sound like shattering glass. "But there's something...off about him. People talk, Snow. They say he's not quite right in the head."

I bristle, a surge of protectiveness rising within me. I don't know why I feel so protective of him, but I do. "I think I can judge his character for myself, thanks."

"Of course, dear. I'm just looking out for you." She reaches out, patting my hand in a gesture that feels more condescending than comforting. "I'd hate to see you get hurt. Men like that...they're nothing but trouble, especially for such an sweet little thing like you."

I pull my hand away, jaw clenched. "I appreciate your concern, but I can handle myself."

Evelyn shrugs, her expression inscrutable. "Suit yourself. But don't say I didn't warn you." She glances at her watch, a delicate gold piece that probably costs more than my rent. "I should be going. Places to be, people to see. You understand."

As she turns to leave, I catch a flicker of movement from the corner of my eye. Evelyn's fingers twist in an intricate pattern, her lips moving soundlessly. A shiver runs down my spine, and for a moment, the air around her seems to shimmer with an otherworldly light.

Then it's gone, and she's sweeping out the door in a swirl of expensive perfume and dark silk. I stand there, heart pounding, trying desperate to figure out just what the fuck is going on.

Four

After work, I head into the nearby forest. Hiking has always helped clear my head, and I've never needed to clear my mind more than I do right now.

But today, something feels different...

The forest envelops me like a living, breathing entity as I follow the winding trail deeper into its heart. Sunlight filters through the canopy of leaves above, casting dappled shadows across my path. The air feels charged with an electricity I can't quite explain, raising the hairs on my arms.

My boots crunch softly on the leaf-strewn ground. I inhale deeply, the earthy scent of moss and rich soil filling my lungs. Normally a hike through these woods soothes my troubled thoughts, but not today. The cryptic warnings in my grandmother's hidden diary echo in my mind, urging me forward in search of answers that continue to elude me.

A twig snaps behind me. I whirl around, heart pounding, but there's no one there. Just the gentle rustling of leaves in the breeze. *Get a grip, Snow. You're letting your imagination run wild.*

I press onward, determination propelling each step. The trees seem to whisper secrets as I pass, their gnarled branches reaching out like ancient fingers. Is it my sleep-deprived mind playing tricks or do their leaves shimmer with an unnatural iridescence?

Without warning, the world tilts on its axis. I stumble, bracing myself against a sturdy oak as a wave of vertigo washes over me. Colors intensify—the greens of the foliage impossibly vibrant, the blue sky above radiant and clear. It's as if a veil has been lifted, revealing the forest's true enchanted nature.

Suddenly, fragments of memories flash before my eyes like a kaleidoscope. Glimpses of my grandmother's gentle smile, the warmth of her embrace. But there are other visions too—unfamiliar and haunting. A raven-haired woman in a flowing crimson dress, her eyes alight with malice. An ornate silver mirror, its surface swirling with mist. And a shimmering red apple, tempting yet deadly.

I gasp, the visions fading as quickly as they appeared. My reflection stares back at me from a nearby pool, pale and shaken. What is happening to me?

The sharp snap of a branch jerks me back to the present. Footsteps approach, heavy and purposeful. My body tenses, ready to flee. A figure emerges from the shadows–a man, clad in dark leather with a crossbow slung across his back. Recognition dawns. It's Garrett, one of my stepmother's most loyal bodyguards. But why is he here?

"Snow," he says, his voice low and urgent. "You need to run. She knows."

"What are you talking about?" I demand, fear coiling in my gut. "Who knows what?"

Garrett glances over his shoulder, as if expecting someone to materialize from the shadows. "Evelyn. She's discovered your true identity, the power you possess. She wants you dead."

"Dead?" I whisper, blood running cold. "But why? I've done nothing to her!"

"It's not about what you've done," Garrett insists. "It's about who you are, Snow. The rightful heir to a legacy she covets. An obstacle to be eliminated."

The weight of his words crashes over me like a

tidal wave. My safe, ordinary life unraveling with each revelation. But amidst the shock, one thing becomes startlingly clear–I am in mortal danger. And if I don't act fast, Evelyn will stop at nothing to destroy me completely.

"Go," Garrett urges, shoving a worn leather satchel into my hands. "Follow the river east until you reach the border of the enchanted wood. There are those who can help you, but you must reach them before Evelyn's forces catch your trail."

"Come with me," I plead, grasping his arm. But he shakes his head sadly.

"I cannot abandon my post. It would raise too much suspicion. But I can buy you time to escape." He cups my cheek gently, his calloused palm rough against my skin. "Be careful, Snow. Trust no one. And never forget–you are far more powerful than you realize."

With those parting words, Garrett melts back into the shadows, leaving me alone once more. I clutch the satchel to my chest, its weight both a comfort and a burden.

I have no choice. Heart racing, I plunge deeper into the mysterious enchanted forest, desperate to outrun the danger snapping at my heels. But even as I flee, one chilling certainty haunts my every step.

Nowhere is safe. Not anymore.

———

Branches claw at my face as I stumble through the underbrush, my breath coming in ragged gasps. The forest seems to close in around me, the trees looming like silent sentinels in the gathering dusk. I've been hiking for hours, but the adrenaline coursing through my veins keeps me moving forward, even as my muscles scream in protest.

Suddenly, I catch a glimmer of light through the dense foliage. Hope flares in my chest, and I quicken my pace, pushing through the last few yards of tangled vines until I emerge into a small clearing.

And there, nestled among the ancient trees, stands a cottage straight out of a fairy tale. Honeysuckle climbs the weathered stone walls, and the windows glow with warm, inviting light. It's like something from a dream—or a distant memory.

Cautiously, I approach the door, my hand trembling as I raise it to knock. But before my knuckles can connect with the wood, the door swings open, revealing a sight that steals the breath from my lungs.

Seven figures stand before me, each more ethereal than the last. They seem to shimmer in the fading light, their features both familiar and alien. The one in the center, a willowy woman with hair the color of moss, steps forward, her eyes glinting with ancient wisdom.

"Welcome, Snow White," she says, her voice echoing with the whispers of a thousand leaves. "We've been expecting you."

I stare at her, my mind reeling. "How...how do you know my name?"

She smiles enigmatically. "We know many things, child. The forest has spoken of your coming."

The others nod in agreement, their gazes both piercing and compassionate. I sense an incredible power emanating from them, a force as old as the earth itself.

"I don't understand," I whisper, my voice trembling. "Who are you? What is this place?"

The woman gestures for me to enter. "Come inside, and all will be revealed. You are safe here, Snow. No harm will befall you within these walls."

I hesitate, my instincts warring with my desperation. But something in her eyes, a glimmer of genuine warmth, makes me take a tentative step forward. As I cross the threshold, a tingling sensation washes over my skin, like I'm passing through an invisible barrier.

The cottage is even more enchanting on the inside, filled with the scent of herbs and honey. The seven beings guide me to a plush armchair by the crackling fireplace, and as I sink into its embrace, I feel the weight of my exhaustion pressing down on me.

"Rest now," the woman murmurs, draping a soft blanket over my lap. "When you wake, your true journey will begin."

My eyelids grow heavy, and I let them drift shut, surrendering to the pull of sleep. But even as I slip into unconsciousness, a flicker of uncertainty dances through my mind.

What secrets does this cottage hold? And am I truly ready to face the truth about my past–and my destiny?

Five

I awaken with a start, my heart pounding as I take in my unfamiliar surroundings. Soft light filters through lace curtains, casting a warm glow on the cozy cottage. The scent of lavender and sage lingers in the air. Where am I?

As I sit up, seven ethereal figures materialize before me, their forms shimmering with an otherworldly radiance.

Then it all comes flooding back to me.

The woods...

The cottage...

I lift my eyes back to the figures. Power emanates from them, ancient and wise. I feel it wash over my skin, raising goosebumps.

The tallest being steps forward, long silver hair

flowing around an ageless face. "Snow White," she says, her melodic voice resonating through my bones. "You have awakened to your true destiny."

I blink in confusion, my mind racing to make sense of this. "My destiny? I don't understand. Who are you?"

"We are the guardians of magic, tasked with guiding those of the bloodline." Another being, draped in shimmering blue robes, fixes me with a penetrating stare. "You, Snow, are the last of your grandmother's lineage. A legacy of powerful good witches."

I shake my head. "So, it's true. I am a witch?"

The silver-haired being smiles patiently. "Ah, but there is so much more to you than that. Magic flows through your veins, even if you have yet to tap into it. Your grandmother was a formidable force for good, standing against the rising tide of darkness."

I think back to Grandma's old diary I found.

"The forces of evil are gathering strength once more," another guardian warns. "Without you to carry on your family's legacy, the world will fall out of balance. You must embrace your power, Snow."

My head spins. A battle against evil? Magical powers? This is all too much. Fear coils in my gut, but beneath it, a flicker of something else—intrigue? Excitement?

I meet the being's luminous gaze. "What if I'm not strong enough? What if I fail? I mean, I don't know anything about magic—or power."

She takes my hand, her touch electric against my skin. "You are stronger than you know. We will guide you, teach you to harness the magic within. But you must have faith in yourself, in the immense power you possess."

Power. The word sends a shiver down my spine. All my life I've felt lost, adrift, searching for purpose. Could this be it? The missing piece clicking into place?

I straighten my shoulders, resolve hardening in my core. "Alright," I say, my voice steady despite the tempest of emotions swirling inside me. "Teach me."

The beings nod in approval, pride shining in their ancient eyes. As they gather closer around me, the air shimmers with barely restrained magic, and I feel it kindling to life inside me—a fire long dormant, now roaring to the surface.

One of the ancient being steps forward, her ethereal form shimmering in the soft light of the cottage. "Close your eyes, Snow," she instructs, her voice a soothing whisper. "Feel the magic thrumming through your veins, pulsing with each heartbeat."

I obey, my eyelids fluttering shut. At first, there's only darkness, the faint sound of my own breathing. But then, gradually, I sense it—a warm, tingling sensation that starts in my fingertips and spreads through my body like wildfire.

"Good," the being murmurs. "Now, repeat after me: 'Lux in tenebris, ignis in sanguine.'"

The words feel foreign on my tongue, but as I speak them, the heat inside me intensifies, concentrating in my palms. "Lux in tenebris, ignis in sanguine," I whisper, my voice trembling with the force of the magic.

Suddenly, my eyes snap open, and I gasp. Hovering above my outstretched hands is a sphere of pure, shimmering light. It pulses in time with my heartbeat, casting a soft glow on the faces of the beings around me.

"Well done, Snow," another being praises, his eyes glinting with satisfaction. "You're a natural."

Pride surges through me, tempered by a flutter of nerves. This power, this magic—it's exhilarating, but also terrifying in its intensity.

The beings guide me through spell after spell, each one more complex than the last. I learn to summon fire and water, to manipulate the elements with a flick of my wrist. The incantations flow more easily now, the gestures becoming second nature.

As I practice, I lose myself in the rhythm of the magic, the world around me fading away until there is only the rush of power, the thrum of energy beneath my skin. In these moments, I feel alive, invigorated, as if I've finally found my true calling.

But doubt still lingers at the edges of my mind, a nagging whisper that I can't quite silence. What if I'm not strong enough to face the evil that threatens our world? What if I let everyone down?

As if sensing my thoughts, the ancient being places a comforting hand on my shoulder. "Remember, Snow," she says softly, "magic is not just about power. It's about intention, about the strength of your heart. Trust in yourself, and you will never fail."

I nod, taking a deep breath. I may not feel ready for this destiny, for the weight of responsibility that rests on my shoulders. But with the guidance of these wise beings and the magic coursing through my veins, I know I have no choice but to try.

The ancient being's words echo in my mind as I face my next challenge. The spell before me is complex, requiring a delicate balance of energy and precision. I close my eyes, focusing inward, feeling the magic swirling within me like a tempest waiting to be unleashed.

I begin the incantation, my voice low and steady. The ancient language feels foreign on my tongue, yet somehow familiar, as if the words have always been a part of me. As I speak, I can feel the power building, the air around me crackling with energy.

But something isn't right. The magic feels unstable, slipping from my grasp like water through my fingers. I falter, my concentration wavering, and suddenly the energy explodes outward in a burst of blinding light.

I'm thrown backwards, landing hard on the ground. Pain lances through my body, and for a moment, I can only lie there, gasping for breath.

"Snow!" The ancient being is at my side in an instant, her voice laced with concern. "Are you alright?"

I nod, wincing as I push myself up into a sitting position. "I'm fine," I say, though my voice trembles slightly. "I just...I couldn't control it."

The being smiles gently, her eyes filled with understanding. "It takes time, Snow. Magic is not something to be mastered overnight. You must be patient with yourself, and remember that even the greatest of witches make mistakes."

I take a deep breath, trying to calm my racing heart. "But what if I can't do it?" I whisper, voicing the fear that has been lurking in the depths of my mind. "What if I'm not strong enough?"

The being takes my hand, her touch warm and reassuring. "You are stronger than you know, Snow. Your magic comes from a place of love, of compassion. That is a power that can never be defeated."

I nod slowly, letting her words sink in. I think of my grandmother, of the legacy she left behind. I think of the people I love, the ones I'm fighting to protect.

"I won't give up," I say firmly, pushing myself to my feet. "I'll keep practicing and learning. I won't let them down."

The ancient being smiles, pride shining in her eyes. "I know you won't, Snow. You have a heart full of courage and a spirit that cannot be broken. Trust in yourself, and you will find the way."

I take a deep breath, squaring my shoulders.

I can do this.

Six

As the days turn into weeks, I find myself falling into a rhythm of magic and self-discovery. Each morning, I wake with the sun, stepping out into the dewy grass to meditate and connect with the energies around me. I can feel the pulse of the earth beneath my feet, the whisper of the wind in my hair. It's as if the world is speaking to me, sharing its secrets one breath at a time.

My training intensifies, the spells growing more complex, the rituals more intricate. I stumble at times, my magic sputtering like a candle in the wind. But I don't let the frustration consume me. Instead, I take a deep breath, centering myself, and try again. And again. And again. Until the spell flows from my fingertips like water, until the energy thrums through my veins like a heartbeat.

The beings watch me with proud smiles, their ancient eyes sparkling with wisdom. They offer guidance when I falter, encouragement when I doubt myself. And slowly, surely, I feel my confidence grow. I am no longer the uncertain girl who arrived at this cottage, but a woman stepping into her power, embracing her destiny.

One evening, as the sun dips below the horizon, painting the sky in hues of orange and pink, I find myself alone in the cottage. The beings have gradually withdrawn, their presence fading like mist in the morning light. A part of me aches at their absence, at the loss of their comforting presence. But another part of me knows that this is how it must be. They have given me the tools, the knowledge, the strength. Now it is up to me to use them.

I step outside, the cool night air kissing my skin. The stars glitter above me, a tapestry of light against the velvet sky. I close my eyes, reaching out with my senses, feeling the magic that flows through everything around me. The rustle of leaves, the hoot of an owl, the whisper of the wind—all of it is alive with energy, with power.

As I step back into the cozy warmth of the

cottage, my gaze is drawn to the far corner of the room. A flicker of candlelight dances across the worn spines of ancient books, their pages whispering secrets of a time long past. Curiosity tugs at me, urging me to explore further.

I run my fingers along the rough-hewn shelves, marveling at the intricate carvings etched into the wood. Each groove tells a story, a tale of magic and wonder. And then, hidden behind a stack of dusty tomes, I find it—a small, ornate box, its surface adorned with symbols I've never seen before.

With trembling hands, I lift the lid, revealing a treasure trove of artifacts. A crystal vial filled with shimmering liquid, a tarnished silver amulet, a bundle of dried herbs tied with a frayed ribbon. Each item hums with power, with a history waiting to be uncovered.

I settle onto the floor, crossing my legs beneath me as I begin to sort through the contents of the box. The soft glow of the candles illuminates the pages of an ancient grimoire, its edges worn and yellowed with age. As I pore over the faded ink, I feel a thrill of excitement running through me.

This is the knowledge of my ancestors, the secrets they left behind for me to discover. Each word, each diagram, each carefully drawn symbol holds the key to unlocking the full potential of my magic. I lose myself in the pages, my mind racing with possibilities.

Hours pass, the candles burning low as I immerse myself in the wisdom of the past. With each new spell, each incantation, I feel a sense of connection to those who came before me. Their strength, their courage, their unwavering belief in the power of magic—all of it flows through me, guiding me forward.

As the first rays of dawn begin to peek through the cottage windows, I close the grimoire with a sense of reverence. I have only scratched the surface of the knowledge hidden within these walls, but already I feel a renewed sense of purpose, a clarity of vision.

The morning sun climbs higher in the sky, and I step out of the cottage and into the surrounding forest. The air is crisp and cool, carrying the scent of pine and damp earth. I take a deep breath, letting the peacefulness of the woods wash over me.

With each step, I feel a sense of connection to the natural world around me. The rustling of leaves, the chittering of squirrels, the gentle babbling of a nearby brook—all of it seems to whisper secrets meant only for my ears. I close my eyes and let my magic reach out, sensing the thrumming energy that pulses through every living thing.

For the first time in longer than I can remember, I feel truly at peace. Here, in the heart of the forest, there are no expectations, no demands, no constant reminders of the dangers that lurk beyond the cottage walls. There is only the quiet solace of nature, the gentle embrace of the earth beneath my feet.

I wander deeper into the woods, my mind drifting to thoughts of the future. Part of me longs to stay here forever, to lose myself in the study of magic and the simplicity of a life lived in harmony with the natural world. But another part of me knows that I cannot hide from my responsibilities forever.

Sooner or later, I will have to return to the city, to the cafe that has been my home and my livelihood for so long. The thought fills me with a sense of dread, a fear that I cannot quite shake. What dangers await me there? What sacrifices will I be forced to make in the name of my magical destiny?

I reach a small clearing and sink to the ground, my back against the rough bark of an ancient oak tree. The doubts and fears swirl within me, threatening to overwhelm me. I have come so far, learned so much, but still I feel uncertain, afraid of what the future may hold.

"I don't know if I'm strong enough," I whisper to the empty air, my voice barely more than a breath. "I don't know if I can do this alone."

As if in answer, a gentle breeze rustles through the leaves above me, carrying with it the faintest hint of a voice. "You are never alone, Snow," it seems to say. "The magic within you is a part of something greater, a force that connects all living things. Trust in it, and it will guide you through even the darkest of times."

I close my eyes and let the words wash over me, feeling a sense of comfort and strength rising within me. I may not have all the answers, but I know that I am not alone. The magic that flows through my veins is a part of something ancient and powerful, a force that has sustained my ancestors for generations.

With a deep breath, I rise to my feet and begin the long walk back to the cottage. The path ahead may be uncertain, but I know that I will face it with courage and determination. I am Snow White, daughter of a long line of powerful witches, and I will not be afraid to embrace my destiny, whatever it may hold.

SEVEN

The gentle breeze rustles the leaves as I step out of the cottage, my heart heavy with the weight of the secrets I've just uncovered. A worn, leather-bound diary presses against my chest, tucked inside my vintage lace blouse. Its pages whisper of a truth that could shatter everything I've ever known.

How Evelyn killed my grandmother and mother before sinking her claws into my father.

All because of me.

To keep me from rising to power so she could stop me from stopping her.

"Hello, dear child." A frail, elderly woman emerges from the shadows, her weathered face partially obscured by a tattered shawl. Despite the warmth of the sun, a shiver runs down my spine.

I force a polite smile. "Good morning. Can I help you with something?"

She hobbles closer, her gnarled fingers clutching a basket. The scent of ripe apples fills the air, sweet and cloying. "I couldn't help but notice your radiant aura, my dear. You possess a rare magical potential."

I tilt my head, curiosity mingling with suspicion. "I'm not sure what you mean."

"Take this." The woman reaches into her basket and produces an apple, its skin a mesmerizing crimson. It seems to pulse with an otherworldly energy. "One bite will fully unlock the power within you."

Uncertainty coils in my stomach as I hesitantly accept the fruit. Its smooth surface is cool against my fingertips. The seven didn't say anything about this...

But maybe they forgot?

I meet the woman's piercing gaze, searching for any hint of deception. But her eyes are pools of emerald green, deep and unfathomable. Something ancient and powerful lurks within their depths.

"What's the catch?" I ask, my voice barely above a whisper.

A flicker of amusement dances across her weathered features. "No catch, my dear. Consider it a gift from one who recognizes your true potential."

I glance down at the apple, its allure growing stronger with each passing second. It seems to call to me.

Unlock your true potential.

Yet a small voice in the back of my mind whispers a warning, urging caution.

I take a deep breath, the scent of magic and danger intertwining in the air. My fingers tighten around the apple as I make my decision. With a mixture of trepidation and resolve, I raise the fruit to my lips, ready to embrace whatever fate awaits me.

The first bite is crisp and sweet, the juice bursting on my tongue like liquid fire. A rush of energy courses through my veins, igniting every nerve ending with a searing intensity. The world around me blurs, colors bleeding together in a kaleidoscope of sensations.

I gasp, the apple tumbling from my grasp as a wave of dizziness washes over me. My knees buckle, and I sink to the ground, my vision fading at the edges. The old woman's face looms above me, a wicked smile playing across her lips.

"Sweet dreams, Snow," she croons, her voice

distorted and echoing in my mind. "Let the curse unfold."

Darkness encroaches, pulling me under like a riptide. As consciousness slips away, a single thought crystallizes in my mind: I've been betrayed. The apple, the old woman, the promise of power—all a deception.

And now, as the poison courses through my veins and the world fades to black, I can only wonder what horrors await me in this cursed slumber. The secrets of my past, the truth of my magic, all lost in an endless void of shadows and silence.

———

The darkness consumes me, a suffocating embrace that pulls me deeper into the abyss. Time loses all meaning, seconds stretching into eternities as I drift through the void. Fragments of memories flicker behind my eyelids, taunting me with glimpses of a life I can no longer reach.

Distantly, I hear voices calling my name, their urgency muffled by the thick veil of the curse. Evan's voice rings out above the rest, raw and desperate. "Snow, please wake up. Don't leave me."

I feel the press of his hand against my cheek, the

warmth of his touch a fleeting anchor in this sea of nothingness. The seven beings gather around me, their worried murmurs a distant hum. They try everything to rouse me—ancient incantations, healing potions, even the touch of a unicorn's horn —but nothing penetrates the dark spell's iron grip.

As my life force ebbs away, the curse tightening its hold, I sense Evan's presence beside me. His breath hitches, a sound of barely contained anguish. "I should have told you the truth from the beginning," he whispers, his voice thick with emotion. "But I was afraid...afraid you wouldn't believe me, afraid you'd turn away."

A single tear falls upon my skin, a searing point of contact in the numbing cold. Evan's words echo in my mind, tantalizing hints of a revelation just beyond my grasp. What truth has he been hiding? What secrets lie buried in the depths of his heart?

But even as the questions burn within me, I feel myself slipping further away, the curse's icy fingers dragging me into an eternal slumber. The voices fade, the sensations dull, until all that remains is the faint beat of my own heart, a fragile reminder of the life I'm losing with each passing moment.

And still, Evan's presence lingers, a desperate plea in the darkness. "I won't let you go, Snow. I'll find a way to break this curse, no matter the cost. I swear it."

His words are the last thing I hear as the void claims me, a final promise that echoes through the endless night. As I surrender to the curse's embrace, I cling to that promise like a lifeline, a glimmer of hope in a world gone dark.

But even hope seems a distant dream now, as the magic weaves its sinister web, trapping me in a prison of my own mind. And so I fall, deeper and deeper, into a sleep from which I may never wake, my fate now resting in the hands of a man whose secrets may be the key to my salvation... or my ultimate undoing.

———

The darkness consumes me, a suffocating void that swallows all light and sound. I drift, lost in an endless sea of nothingness, my consciousness fading like a distant dream. But even in this abyss, I feel a flicker of warmth, a presence that refuses to let me go.

Evan's voice pierces through the haze, a desperate whisper that echoes in the depths of my mind. "Snow, please, come back to me. I can't lose you, not like this."

His words stir something within me, a faint

glimmer of recognition amidst the darkness. I struggle to respond, to reach out and grasp the lifeline he offers, but the curse's hold is too strong, its icy tendrils pulling me further into oblivion.

And yet, Evan persists, his voice growing stronger, more urgent. "I should have told you the truth from the beginning, Snow. I'm not just a traveler, not just a man with a mysterious past. I'm a prince, cursed to wander this world until I find the one who can break the spell."

The revelation sends a shockwave through my fading consciousness, a burst of clarity in the fog of enchanted sleep. A prince? Cursed? The pieces of the puzzle begin to fall into place, the strange connection between us, the inexplicable pull that drew me to him from the very start.

"I was sent to protect you, Snow, to guide you towards your destiny. But somewhere along the way, I fell in love with you, truly and deeply. And now, I fear that love may not be enough to save you."

His confession ignites a spark within me, a flicker of hope that refuses to be extinguished. I cling to it, desperately, fighting against the curse's relentless pull. If Evan's love is true, if the bond between us is as strong as I believe, then perhaps there is still a chance, a way to break free from this never-ending nightmare.

But doubt creeps in, insidious and cold. How can I be sure that our love is real, that it's powerful enough to overcome the dark magic that threatens to tear us apart? I've been betrayed before, my trust shattered by those I held dear. Can I truly put my faith in Evan, in a man whose secrets run deeper than I ever imagined?

As I wrestle with these thoughts, the curse tightens its grip, dragging me further into the abyss. The warmth of Evan's presence begins to fade, his voice growing distant and muffled. I try to hold on, to anchor myself to the world of the living, but the darkness is too strong, too all-consuming.

And so I slip away, falling deeper into the enchanted slumber, my doubts and fears swirling like a tempest within my mind. As the last vestiges of consciousness fade, I'm left with a single, desperate thought: if our love is true, if it's strong enough to break the curse, then Evan will find a way to bring me back, to rescue me from this eternal night.

But if not, if our bond is nothing more than a fleeting dream, then I fear I may be lost forever, trapped in a world of shadows and silence, forever beyond the reach of those who once loved me.

Eight

Evan

The ancient oak trees sway, their leaves whispering secrets as I step into the enchanted forest. A shiver runs down my spine, but I push forward, determined. I need to find them—the seven mystical beings who hold the key to saving Snow.

As I venture deeper, the air grows thick with anticipation. Suddenly, a voice echoes through the trees. "Evan, you've come at last."

I spin around to see a glowing figure emerge from the shadows. One of the seven. "I need your help," I say, my voice steady despite the fear gripping my heart.

The being nods solemnly. "We know why you're here. The prophecy...and Snow." It gestures for me to follow. "Come, the others are waiting."

We weave through the dense foliage until we reach a clearing bathed in ethereal light. Six more figures await, their forms shimmering with ancient magic. My breath catches. This is it—my last chance to save her.

"Evelyn's power grows by the minute," one of them warns. "She will stop at nothing to destroy Snow before the prophecy is fulfilled."

I clench my fists, anger and determination surging through me. Memories of my past, of the secrets I've kept, flood my mind. But I push them aside. All that matters now is Snow.

"I'm ready to do whatever it takes," I declare, my voice ringing with conviction. "Even if it means sacrificing everything."

The beings exchange knowing glances. "Very well," their leader says. "Then let us begin. We must rally our allies from across the forest. Evelyn's assault will be swift and merciless."

As they disperse to gather reinforcements, I close my eyes and picture Snow's face—her porcelain skin, raven hair, those striking blue eyes that see into my soul. I've tried to keep my distance, to protect her from my past and my own darkness. But I can't deny the connection between us, the undeniable pull.

Hang on, Snow, I silently plead. *I'm coming for you. No matter the cost.*

———

Miles away, in the depths of her lair, Evelyn Blackwood smiles wickedly as she gazes into a swirling crystal orb. "Oh, Evan," she purrs, her emerald eyes flashing. "Always the hero, aren't you? But you're too late."

With a wave of her elegant hand, dark tendrils of magic erupt from the orb, snaking through the air. "Let the games begin," she whispers, her velvety voice dripping with malice.

The tendrils shoot through the forest, closing in on the cottage where Snow lies trapped in cursed slumber. Trees wither and creatures scatter in their wake, the very fabric of nature recoiling from Evelyn's poisonous power.

As the attack reaches the cottage, a shimmering dome of light springs up around it—a protective shield woven by the seven beings. But Evelyn's assault is relentless, the dark magic crashing against the barrier like a raging tide.

Inside, Snow stirs, her brow furrowing as if sensing the impending danger. But the curse holds her deep in its grasp, oblivious to the battle raging outside.

———

I race through the forest, my heart hammering against my ribcage. *Hold on, Snow. Hold on.* As I burst into the clearing around the cottage, I'm met with a scene of pure chaos—Evelyn's dark magic pummeling the shield, the seven beings straining to maintain it.

Our eyes lock across the maelstrom of power. Evelyn's lips curve into a wicked smile. "Welcome to the end, Evan," she hisses. "Say goodbye to your precious Snow."

Raw determination surges through my veins. Not a chance, witch. Gritting my teeth, I plunge into the heart of the battle, my own dormant magic awakening to protect the woman I love. For Snow, I will risk it all. No matter what haunts me from my shadowed past, I will be her light.

I push through the onslaught, every step a battle

against the dark magic that tears at me. The air crackles with raw power, the ground trembling beneath my feet. But I don't falter. I can't. Snow needs me.

Evelyn's laughter rings out, cruel and mocking. "Foolish prince! You think your love can save her? You're nothing but a cursed beast, unworthy of a happy ending."

Her words slice into me, echoing the doubts that have plagued me for so long. But as I look to the cottage, to where Snow lies trapped in an unending sleep, I find a strength I never knew I had. "You're wrong, Evelyn," I growl, my voice raw with emotion. "Love is the most powerful magic of all."

With a final surge of energy, I break through the shield, the protective magic parting before me like a shimmering curtain. I stumble into the cottage, my breath coming in ragged gasps. There, on a bed of soft furs, lies Snow, her raven hair fanned out like a dark halo, her skin as pale as the moon.

I drop to my knees beside her, my hand trembling as I brush a lock of hair from her face. "Snow," I whisper, my voice cracking. "I'm here. I'm sorry it took me so long."

The battle still rages outside, the cottage walls shuddering under the onslaught. But in this moment, there is only us. Gently, I cup her face in my hands, my heart aching with a love so fierce it steals my breath. "I am you prince, Snow. We loved each other in another lifetime. You just don't remember, but I do. I remember every glance, every touch, everything about you. And I'd give my life to save yours. I love you, Snow White. Come back to me."

And then, as if the world itself is holding its breath, I press my lips to hers in a kiss born of desperation and unwavering love. A kiss that carries the weight of a thousand unspoken promises. A kiss that will either be our salvation...or our final goodbye.

As our lips meet, a blinding light explodes outward, filling the cottage with a radiance that chases away every shadow. I feel the curse that has held me captive for so long shatter, the weight of it lifting from my soul. And then, a miracle.

Snow's eyes flutter open, a soft gasp escaping her lips. "Evan?" she breathes, her voice tinged with wonder.

Tears of joy stream down my face as I gather her into my arms, holding her close. "It's me, Snow. I'm here. And I'll never let you go again."

Outside, Evelyn's screams of rage pierce the air as her dark magic dissipates. I help Snow sit up, and then she rises, a look of determination in her eyes.

"This ends now," she states firmly as she heads resolutely for the door.

Snow strides purposefully towards the cottage door, her hand outstretched, a soft white glow emanating from her palm. I follow close behind, ready to support her, to face this final battle together. As we step outside, the chaos of the magical assault engulfs us—dark tendrils lashing out, the ground quaking beneath our feet. But Snow doesn't falter.

She raises her hand, and a pulse of pure, radiant energy surges forth, pushing back against Evelyn's malevolent magic. The air shimmers with the clash of opposing forces, light battling against darkness in a dizzying display of power. Snow's brow furrows with concentration, her eyes blazing with an inner fire as she pours every ounce of her strength into the fight.

Evelyn's eyes widen in disbelief as Snow's magic grows stronger, the white light intensifying until it's almost blinding. "No!" she shrieks, her voice raw with fury and desperation. "This cannot be! I am the most powerful sorceress in the land!"

But Snow's magic is unyielding, fueled by the purity of her heart and the love that binds us together. The dark tendrils begin to wither and retreat, unable to withstand the onslaught of Snow's radiant power. The seven mystical beings join their strength with hers, weaving their ancient magic into the tapestry of light that surrounds us.

Evelyn's screams grow more desperate as the light closes in around her, her once-regal features twisting with rage and fear. "You will pay for this, Snow White!" she spits, her emerald eyes flashing with venom. "I will have my revenge!"

Snow shakes her head, her expression a mix of pity and resolve. "No, Evelyn," she says softly, her voice carrying an undeniable authority. "Your reign of darkness ends here. You will never again harm those I love."

With a final, magnificent surge of power, Snow's magic envelops Evelyn completely, the light so bright it's nearly impossible to look at directly. Evelyn's shrieks fade into silence as the light cocoons her, sealing her away in a prison of her own making. As the glow slowly dissipates, all that remains is a small, pulsing orb of darkness, suspended in mid-air.

Snow reaches out and grasps the orb, her touch causing it to shudder and shrink. "Your darkness will no longer cast a shadow over this land, Evelyn Blackwood," she declares, her voice ringing with finality. "From this day forward, you will be banished to the realm of shadows, where your power can never again threaten those who walk in the light."

With a flick of her wrist, Snow sends the orb hurtling into the sky, where it vanishes among the stars, forever sealed away from the world of the living.

As the orb vanishes into the heavens, a hush falls over the enchanted forest. The trees seem to exhale a collective sigh of relief, their leaves rustling gently in the warm breeze. The seven mystical beings bow their heads in reverence, their shimmering forms flickering with exhaustion but also with triumph.

I step forward and take Snow's hand in mine, our fingers intertwining as if they were always meant to be joined. She turns to me, her striking blue eyes brimming with emotions—relief, love, and a hint of uncertainty.

"Evan," she whispers, her voice trembling slightly. "Is it really over? Is Evelyn truly gone?"

I pull her close, wrapping my arms around her slender frame, feeling the warmth of her body against mine. "Yes, my love," I murmur, pressing a gentle kiss to her forehead. "You did it. You saved us all."

Snow leans into my embrace, her head resting on my chest. "I couldn't have done it without you," she says softly. "Your love, your sacrifice...it broke the curse and gave me the strength I needed."

I tilt her chin up, gazing deeply into her eyes. "Snow, I would do anything for you. I have loved you across lifetimes, even when I didn't fully understand why. You are my destiny, my heart, my everything."

Tears glisten in her eyes as she rises on her tiptoes, her lips meeting mine in a kiss that holds the promise of a future together. The kiss deepens, our mouths moving in perfect synchrony, as if we have been lovers for centuries. Heat courses through my veins, my heart pounding with a desire that has been building since the moment I first laid eyes on her.

As we finally pull apart, breathless and flushed, the seven beings approach us, their expressions a mix of joy and solemnity. "Snow White, Evan," their leader addresses us, "you have fulfilled the prophecy and vanquished the darkness that threatened our land. Your love has proven to be the most powerful magic of all."

Snow and I exchange a glance, our hearts full to bursting. "What happens now?" Snow asks, her hand still clasped tightly in mine.

The being smiles, a twinkle in its ancient eyes. "Now, you live. You love. You rule this kingdom together, as equals, as partners. The land will prosper under your guidance, and your love will be a shining beacon for all to see."

I turn to Snow, my heart swelling with adoration and hope. "Together," I say, my voice thick with emotion. "Always."

She nods, her smile brighter than the sun itself. "Always," she echoes, sealing our vow with another kiss.

Which I waste no time deepening as my cock lenghtens in my pants.

I need to claim my princess again. "That one time in the coffee shop wasn't enough," I growl as I pull her flush against me.

"I almost thought it was a dream," she says breathily as I feel her nipples pebble through our clothing.

Snow pulls back slightly, her eyes darkening with desire as she feels the evidence of my arousal pressed against her. "That was no dream, my princess," I tell her as my hand trails over her hip. "I was deep inside you right where I belong."

She squeals as I scoop her into my arms and carry her back to the cottage, leaving the seven mystical beings to begin restoring balance to the enchanted forest. Once inside, the air between us crackles with anticipation, the intensity of our long-denied passion threatening to consume us both.

Unable to hold back a moment longer, I capture Snow's lips in a searing kiss, pouring every ounce of my love and longing into the embrace. She responds with equal fervor, her fingers tangling in my hair as she presses her lithe body against mine. We stumble towards the bed, our hands roaming, desperate to touch, to feel, to reassure ourselves that this is real.

Clothing is shed in a frenzied rush, scattered across the floor as we tumble onto the soft furs. I take a moment to drink in the sight of Snow laid bare before me, her porcelain skin flushed, her raven hair fanned out like a dark halo. "You are so beautiful," I whisper reverently, my fingers skimming along the curves of her body.

Snow arches into my touch, her breathing shallow. "Evan, please," she whimpers, her hips rolling against mine in a silent plea.

I answer her call, covering her body with my own, the heat of our skin igniting an inferno within us both. We move together in a dance as old as time itself, our bodies fitting together like missing pieces of a puzzle. Each gasp, each moan, each whisper of devotion drives us higher, the intensity building until it crests in a blinding wave of ecstasy.

In the aftermath, we lie tangled together, our limbs entwined, hearts beating as one. Snow traces lazy patterns on my chest, her touch soothing and electric all at once. "I love you, Evan," she murmurs, her voice soft with sated contentment.

I press a tender kiss to her temple, my arms tightening around her. "And I love you, Snow. Forever and always."

NINE

The walk back to "The Poisoned Apple" passes in a blur, my mind still reeling, processing, grappling with the enormity of what transpired. As we approach the familiar red brick exterior, ivy-covered and inviting as always, a strange sense of peace settles over me.

Inside, the rich aroma of coffee grounds and old books embraces us like an old friend. Late afternoon sunlight slants through the stained-glass windows, casting kaleidoscope colors across the worn hardwood floors. The coffee shop is the same, yet different

There's still coffee, but now there are also shelves lined with leather-bound tomes and glass jars filled with shimmering powders and dried herbs that exude magic.

But it's the clientele that makes me pause. Fairies perched atop the espresso machine, gossiping over thimbles of nectar. A grumpy troll hunched in the corner, sipping a gigantic mug of something mossy and pungent. Pixies zipping to and fro like caffeinated hummingbirds. This place has become a sanctuary.

And I'm its guardian now. No longer the lost princess trapped under the thumb of a wicked stepmother, but a woman who has stepped into her own power. It's daunting and exhilarating in equal measure.

"Quite the kingdom you've inherited here, Snow," Evan muses, pride sparkling in his emerald eyes as he takes in the menagerie of magical patrons.

"Our kingdom," I correct him with a sly smile. Unspoken promise and possibility hang in the air between us, the start of something new. "Now, let's get to work, my prince. Coffee to brew, curses to break, damsels and dudes to save. All in a day's work."

————

As the sun dips below the horizon, the last of our otherworldly patrons take their leave in a shimmer of fairy dust and the faint echo of fluttering wings. Evan locks the door with a flick of his wrist, ancient runes flaring to life to ward and protect.

The air takes on a different quality, charged with an undercurrent of anticipation and hunger that has little to do with coffee or pastries. Evan prowls towards me, a wolf stalking his mate, green eyes glittering with intent.

"Alone at last," he rumbles, trailing a finger down my cheek, my neck, igniting sparks in his wake. "I thought they'd never leave."

"Patience is a virtue," I tease, even as I lean into his touch, craving more. Always more.

"And you, my queen, are a temptation."

In a heartbeat, he has me pressed against the wall, his body a delicious weight pinning me in place. I gasp as his lips find my neck, trailing open-mouthed kisses that send shivers racing down my spine. My hands slip beneath his shirt, mapping the sculpted planes of his back, nails digging in as he nips at my collarbone.

Magic swirls around us, responding to the call of our desire. It tugs at our clothes until we are skin to skin, fills the air with the heady perfume of night-blooming flowers. The world narrows to Evan's wicked mouth, his clever fingers, the press of his body against mine.

"I need you," I breathe against his lips, a plea and a command. "Now."

With a growl, he hoists me up, my legs wrapping around his waist as he carries me to the worn velvet sofa by the crackling fireplace. He lays me down like an offering, eyes dark with lust and devotion.

"As my queen commands."

Then his mouth is on me, worshipping every inch with lips and tongue and teeth until I am trembling, incoherent, consumed by pleasure and need. When he finally slides into me, two puzzle pieces clicking into place, I nearly sob with relief. We move together, urgently chasing our release, magic crackling over our skin like static. Pressure coils tighter and tighter low in my belly until it shatters, my cry of ecstasy mingling with Evan's rough groan.

Spent and sated, we lay tangled together, trading lazy kisses as our heartbeats slow.

This is just the beginning of our happily ever after, and I can't wait to see what the next chapter holds.

. . .

Don't miss the rest of the Spicy Romantasy series! Go to www.authorkenzieskye.com to find out where to get the rest of the series and to get a free book!